ONCE
UPON A
CRIME

Anne Schraff

PAGETURNERS

SUSPENSE
Boneyard
The Cold, Cold Shoulder
The Girl Who Had Everything
Hamlet's Trap
Roses Red as Blood

DETECTIVE
The Case of the Bad Seed
The Case of the Cursed Chalet
The Case of the Dead Duck
The Case of the Wanted Man
The Case of the Watery Grave

ADVENTURE
A Horse Called Courage
Planet Doom
The Terrible Orchid Sky
Up Rattler Mountain
Who Has Seen the Beast?

SCIENCE FICTION
Bugged!
Escape from Earth
Flashback
Murray's Nightmare
Under Siege

MYSTERY
The Hunter
Once Upon a Crime
Whatever Happened to
  Megan Marie?
When Sleeping Dogs Awaken
Where's Dudley?

SPY
A Deadly Game
An Eye for an Eye
I Spy, e-Spy
Scavenger Hunt
Tuesday Raven

ISBN-13: 978-1-56254-179-8
ISBN-10: 1-56254-179-X
eBook: 978-1-60291-221-2

Printed in the U.S.A.

19 18 17 16 15   8 9 10 11 12

CONTENTS

Chapter 1 5

Chapter 2 11

Chapter 3 20

Chapter 4 28

Chapter 5 33

Chapter 6 40

Chapter 7 46

Chapter 8 54

Chapter 9 60

Chapter 10 67

Chapter 1

Vivi Calderon was doing library research for her ancient history class at City College. One day she grew so sleepy that her head was nodding over a book about Crete. Then something peculiar caught her eye and jolted her to attention.

A middle-aged man at a nearby table was frantically thumbing through a pile of books. He was riffling, page by page, through one book after another—but much too quickly to be reading anything. It was a very strange sight, especially since the man actually looked *possessed*. His hair was disheveled and his eyes were wild. But in contrast, he was very well dressed in an Italian silk suit that looked a little old and worn.

Vivi had come to the downtown library with her friend, Jamal Grey. Now she left her table and went to find Jamal. She tapped him on the shoulder as he was taking a book from the stacks.

"What's up, Vivi?" Jamal asked.

"I want you to come over to my table and take a look at this oddball guy," Vivi whispered. "It's just so weird!"

Jamal and Vivi returned to the table where her books on ancient history were piled. They both sat down and pretended to be reading books as they watched the man from the corners of their eyes.

"What do you think he's doing?" Vivi asked quietly.

Jamal shrugged and grinned. "Must be a real speed reader! Boy, that dude can read faster than I can blink!"

"I'm serious, Jamal! What do you think he's *really* doing?" Vivi asked.

"Maybe he thinks somebody stashed some money in one of those old books.

Maybe he's trying to find it," Jamal said. "One time I read about an eccentric old guy who *did* hide money in books. It was his weird way of getting people to read them."

Suddenly the man looked up. He had heard the young people whispering in the otherwise silent room. Now he reached up to smooth down strands of his unkempt black hair. When he looked over at Vivi and Jamal, his burning black eyes reminded Vivi of an eagle's piercing gaze. The man's eyes drilled into the young couple like a laser.

"Quick—pretend you're reading," Vivi whispered. "Don't let him see you looking at him!"

"He's sure a *mean* looking dude, huh?" Jamal whispered back.

Finally, the man returned his attention to his own stack of books. From time to time Vivi stole a glance at him. Twice she caught him staring back at her. His suspicions had been aroused.

He knew that Vivi was watching him, and that made Vivi nervous.

"I'm out of here," Vivi said, getting up. "That guy gives me the creeps. I'm checking out these two books and then I'm leaving." Vivi walked to the desk with Jamal right behind her. She checked out a book on Athens and one on Crete.

As Vivi and Jamal walked home, the fog that would end up pea-soup thick later in the evening was already casting a blurry haze. Vivi liked the fog. The neighborhood was past its prime, filled with aging apartment buildings and tacky mini-malls. To Vivi, the fog provided a welcome cover. She and Jamal both lived in an old apartment building on the corner. Vivi lived on the second floor, Jamal on the fourth.

"Wow, Jamal, wouldn't it be cool if there really *was* money stuck in some of these musty old books?" Vivi said. "It would sure help us out if I brought home some cash along with these musty old books on the Greeks!" Vivi's mother was a hard-working computer technician trying to raise three children on her own. Vivi, the oldest, was now a college student. The two younger boys were still in elementary school.

"Dream on, girl," Jamal laughed. "Rich guys like to *spend* their money— not hide it in library books."

"Yeah," Vivi said, "I'm earning my tuition at the pizza parlor. But with the high cost of clothes and stuff, I can't help Mom very much. I know she's doing without things she needs."

"Yeah, I hear you," Jamal said. "My parents *both* work and we're hurting bad at the end of the month, too. Money doesn't stretch very far when you're feeding three hungry kids."

Just then a strange, creepy feeling came over Vivi. She glanced back. A man who looked like that guy in the library was walking behind them. Were they being followed?

"Jamal," Vivi said quietly, "when we get to the intersection, let's cross the street to see if that guy is really following us. I'm sure it's that weirdo we saw in the library!"

Jamal glanced back and nodded. "Yeah, it's him for sure. Mighty strange that he leaves just when *we* leave, huh?"

Vivi and Jamal crossed the street. The man did the same.

"Let's duck in the deli up ahead. We can wait there for a minute to see if he goes by," Vivi said.

Vivi and Jamal went into the deli. They pretended to study the pink and gray sausage rolls and the huge chunks of cheese. But they were really watching the front window to see if the man would pass by. He didn't.

Did that mean he'd gone off in another direction—or had he, too, ducked in somewhere to wait?

Chapter 2

When Vivi stepped out of the deli, she looked around. "I don't see him anywhere, Jamal. I guess maybe he *wasn't* following us after all," she said.

"Good," Jamal said. "I wouldn't feel too good about a weird old boy like that bird dogging me."

"Me neither. I've got enough on my mind. I need to write this humongous, stupid report on the people of Athens and Crete—you know, comparing their civilizations," Vivi said.

"Didn't you find anything about that on the Internet?" Jamal asked.

"Yeah, but I still needed these old books, and I couldn't find them anywhere but in the big downtown library," Vivi said. "Our college library doesn't have that much on the Greeks."

Unlike Vivi, Jamal didn't go to college. He worked full time at the supermarket. Sometimes he talked about going to college, but his family really needed the money he made.

Vivi went toward her apartment and Jamal went to his. In the old days, their apartment building had been a pretty nice hotel. Then it was remade into apartments. They weren't *bad* exactly, but Vivi had always dreamed of living in a house with green grass and flower beds near the sidewalk.

Actually, Vivi hated *many* things about the apartment—but most of all she hated the lack of a yard where she could sit under a tree with her dream dog. She wasn't even allowed to have a dog in the apartment. Vivi hated the smells in the building, too. Everything that was ever cooked on the second floor seemed to linger in the hall— fish, chicken, onions, broccoli, cabbage—

and the mix of odors hung in a stale, sickening vapor.

Vivi's mom was still at work. She put in a lot of overtime and was happy to do it. Every penny counted.

"Hi, guys! Say, have you two already finished your homework?" Vivi asked her twin ten-year-old brothers.

"Maybe, maybe not. You ain't our mom," Pedro shot back.

"Yeah. Quit trying to be the boss around here," Luis agreed.

The boys resented it when Vivi tried to show authority in Mom's absence. "I'm just trying to make sure you're doing what Mom wants," Vivi said. Then she walked into the kitchen and called out, "I don't suppose either of you geniuses peeled any potatoes for dinner or cut up a salad. . . . "

"That's *your* job, 'cause you're a girl," Pedro retorted, snickering at his brother.

"Boy, have you got a lot to learn," Vivi sighed. "The way it is these days, you little jokers, whoever has the time does the cooking—or maybe the cooking doesn't get done at all."

Pedro got up to get a cola from the refrigerator. Vivi jumped in front of the door. "You know the rules. No colas before dinner. You can have a can of soda during dinner, but not before."

"But Mom makes us drink milk when we eat," Pedro groaned.

"Awww, mean old Mom," Vivi laughed mockingly. "She's just like the wicked witch of the west in that *Wizard of Oz* movie, isn't she?"

"Hey, Luis," Pedro called out as he passed the window. "Who's that dude across the street? Why's he staring up here? Do we owe him money or something?"

Startled, Vivi stopped peeling potatoes and joined her brothers at the window. The fog was really rolling in now, but she could clearly see that the man from the library was standing across the street staring up at *this* window. "That guy was in the library today," Vivi gasped. "He was paging through books real fast like he was looking for something. I *thought* he followed me home—I guess he did. Wow! What could he be doing here?"

"What was he looking for in the old books?" Pedro asked curiously. "Old books got nothing in them but dust and sometimes crushed bugs."

"Yeah, one time I found a silverfish in our dictionary," Luis said, grinning as if that had been a great discovery.

"I have no idea what he was looking for," Vivi said, "but I hate that he knows where I live! He really makes chills go up my spine. The guy's got *awful* eyes— like a vulture or something!"

"*Cool*," Pedro said in admiration. "Maybe he's a secret agent."

"Or maybe he's a hit man," Luis suggested. "But I guess a hit man wouldn't be stupid enough to stand right across the street gawking at us."

As darkness fell, it became too foggy to see much across the street. But Vivi thought she saw the man walking away.

Vivi never mentioned the man to her mother. The woman had enough worries already. Besides, there was probably nothing to it. Maybe the man was just one of the many downtown residents who lived on the fringes of life. Such people were generally harmless. They lived in their own little worlds and they did odd things like spend all day at the library, in the courthouse, or riding the trolleys back and forth.

After dinner, Vivi started reading one of her books. She found out that both Athens and Crete were pretty well civilized. But life on the island of Crete was a lot more fun. Even though Crete was an ancient place, the girls wore pretty dresses and elegant shoes. Life seemed happy and carefree there.

Then, as Vivi turned one of the

pages, a piece of notepaper with a violet pattern tumbled out into her lap.

As usual he was dreadful at dinner. Embarrassed me in front of the Beaumonts. He delights in humiliating me. Oh, what a bed of pain I have made for myself!

At the end of the note was the single initial *M*.

Vivi was shocked by the note. Was it a girl complaining about her boyfriend? Or maybe a wife griping about her husband? What a strange thing to find in a dusty old book about the Greeks!

Vivi put the note back. Maybe it was a joke. Some student like herself was trying to liven up a boring assignment by hiding cryptic notes in a book!

The next day Vivi went alone to the library to get more books. The books she had checked out the day before had not given her enough information to write a good report. Her history teacher,

Ms. Grassville, had said that much of the final grade would depend on this report.

* * *

Vivi wished that Jamal could have come with her, but he was working late at the market. Now, at the library, Vivi was almost afraid to look around. What if she saw the strange man again? She took three books down from the stacks and carried them to a table.

Noticing the room was empty, Vivi sighed with relief. Then, when she was checking the indexes of the books, a cold, uncomfortable feeling came over her. Her skin pricked and tingled. She had the unmistakable feeling that she was being *watched*.

Vivi glanced nervously over at the table where she had seen the man before. And sure enough, there he sat, with five books beside him. Again he was turning the pages obsessively. Vivi watched him. Each time he finished searching a book, he'd look around to make sure the librarian wasn't looking. Then he'd grasp the covers of the book and shake it violently. It looked like he was trying to dislodge something that might be stuck between the pages. Such treatment did the books no good, but he seemed determined not to miss anything.

Vivi concentrated on her own books, rapidly checking them so she could get out of there fast. She was just starting to get up when the man suddenly got up, too. In a panic, Vivi felt blood rushing to her head. He was actually coming over to talk to her!

As he drew closer, Vivi noticed how ghastly the man looked. There was a terrible pallor about him, as if he'd been living in a dank cellar for the last five years and had never seen a ray of sunshine. Actually, she thought . . . he looked like a dead man.

Chapter 3

"Excuse me, miss," the man said in a pleasant, deep voice, "but I see you share my fascination with the Greeks."

Vivi started to speak, but she was so rattled that her voice came out in an embarrassing high-pitched squeak. "I'm a college student. I have to write a report on Greece—you know, Athens and Crete."

"Oh, I see," he said. "Well, I've always been fascinated by the Greeks. Are you aware that they quite literally discovered everything there was to discover? They knew it all before the technology existed to prove their conclusions. Tell me, have you checked out *many* books on the Greeks?"

"Uh . . . just these, and a couple more yesterday," Vivi said.

The man placed his hand over Vivi's. His touch was abnormally cold. More chills went zinging up Vivi's arms. "I wonder if you would do me a favor?" he said. "Could I borrow those books you have there? I promise to return them tomorrow."

"But I need to take them home to write my report," Vivi said.

"It would be very good of you to let me have them *now*. Then, later this afternoon, I could bring them to your apartment. *I know where you live,* and could easily drop them off," the man said.

His eyes seemed to burn into Vivi's face. He reached out, clutching at the books almost desperately. "All right," Vivi said, "you can have them. Don't bother bringing them to my apartment, though. Just bring them back to the library, and I'll get them tomorrow."

Vivi got up to leave, but the man grasped her arm, delaying her. His fingers felt like pincers on her arm. "I have just finished two wonderful books on Greece. Here—you can have them for your report. I'm all done with them," he said pleasantly.

"Oh, thank you," Vivi said with a weak smile. All she could think about was how to get out of there and away from this frightening man. But he didn't let go of her arm right away.

"The books you have at home," he said anxiously, "are you bringing them back tomorrow?"

"Why . . . yes," Vivi said.

"Tell me, did you go through them carefully?" he asked. Vivi had never seen such maniacal eyes. He looked like a madman.

"They . . . uh . . . didn't have what I wanted. I just looked in the index," Vivi lied.

"I see. Well, will you be sure to bring them back tomorrow?" he asked. He seemed relieved when Vivi said she would. Finally, he let go of her arm and

Vivi raced to check out the two books he had given her. They were probably useless for her project, but she was frantic to get out the door.

As Vivi hurried home, she kept looking behind her, but the man wasn't following her. Why should he be? As he said, he already knew where she lived. Vivi rushed past the twins, who were watching a TV sitcom and laughing their heads off.

She quickly went to the two books she had checked out the day before. Obviously, the man was afraid that she had found what he had been looking for in those books.

But what could it be? Money? Stock certificates? Or that silly little violet note? Vivi opened the book on Crete. Now she noticed these words on the title page:

Donated to the City Library from the collection of Lulu Margaret Foster, Grecophile.

A *Grecophile* was a person who loved Greek things, Vivi knew. Maybe the man's mother was Lulu Foster. Maybe she had donated the family books to the library. Maybe the guy needed to find an important document that he had hidden in one of them.

Vivi started going through the book one page at a time—just like the man had been doing—but it was too time consuming. So she carefully shook the pages. A few crushed bugs fell out, along with an old bookmark. Surely that man didn't want that old bookmark!

Then Vivi shook the book once more, and this time another piece of notepaper with the same violet pattern fluttered out. With trembling hands, Vivi picked it up and read it:

How much longer must I suffer? He will be the death of me yet. I want to leave him, but I cannot. My mother says I have made my bed and now I must lie in it. I fear it shall become my deathbed. I want him to pay. He must not escape punishment!

Like the other note, it was signed only with the letter *M*.

Now Vivi felt like she was invading someone's privacy. These notes almost looked like pages from a *diary*. She was sorry she had ever found them. She didn't want to know anything about some terrible tragedy that happened years ago.

Could *M* possibly be that frightening man's wife? Had something dreadful happened to her? Vivi felt a slight shudder go through her body.

The other book on the Greeks had not been donated by Lulu Foster, so Vivi decided not to look at that one. She returned the note to the first book, and then stuffed both books in her backpack. Early the next morning she would return them to the library.

That evening, Vivi and Jamal went down the block to the Spaghetti Shop for a bite to eat.

Vivi told Jamal about the books and the notes. "It seems that this lady, Lulu Margaret Foster, donated books to the library. She must have hidden these notes in some of them, I guess."

"Oh, boy, *Lulu Margaret Foster*," Jamal repeated, "what a funny name."

Jess Hogan, the waitress at the Spaghetti Shop, picked up on the name. "What're you kids talking about Lulu Foster for?" she asked.

Vivi looked up in surprise. "Do you *know* something about her, Jess?" she asked excitedly.

"Oh, sure, she was a big time rich lady—a patron of the arts and all that. She's dead, though. Died about three years ago. Lotta tragedy in that family. The daughter-in-law died in an accident. They weren't *sure* it was an accident right away. At first they thought it was murder. They questioned the husband, but then they let him go. Don't you kids remember that? It was a big story."

"I'm not sure. I guess maybe I remember something about it," Vivi said, "but I didn't pay much attention to it. What was the wife's name?"

Jess grinned. "Aw, that's easy— *Melissa*. Such a pretty name. Her picture was in all the papers. She was beautiful. Poor little Melissa. Took a nasty fall and broke her neck—just like Humpty Dumpty."

Chapter 4

Vivi felt numb. The notes were signed *M*. Was the *M* for *Melissa*? For a minute she was speechless. Then she looked at the waitress and said, "How did the fall happen?"

Jess seemed happy to talk about the incident. After all, what was more fun than intrigue among the rich—especially when murder might be involved? "Well, they had a big staircase, and one day she just tumbled down, head over heels. There were rumors that she and her husband weren't getting along. He was something of a jerk. Some said he just gave her a good push and put an end to her. But nobody could ever prove that," Jess said.

"What was the husband's name?

Do you remember?" Vivi asked.

Jess smiled, proud that she could recall all the details so well. "His name was Barry—Barry Foster."

"What did he look like? Did you ever see a picture of him?" Vivi asked.

"Oh, his picture was in the papers many times. As I remember, he was quite a nice-looking man," Jess said.

"Did he have these really weird, burning eyes?" Vivi asked.

Jess laughed. "Nah. His eyes didn't look any different from anybody else's, as far as I could tell. Of course, he had a big beard and long hair. Never could see why a pretty little rich girl like Melissa married him. She had dated Conan Braxton, the playwright, and he was *so* handsome! Melissa seemed like a flighty girl. Lord knows she had plenty of beaus. But then she settled on a lazy guy with a rich mama. . . . "

As Vivi and Jamal walked home, Jamal said, "That weird guy in the library is probably like Jess—just some little nobody who got caught up in the celebrity story. Look how excited Jess was! And that story had *nothing* to do with *her* life! Probably the library guy just accidentally stumbled on these books donated by the old rich lady. Then he got all excited and started imagining that he had some part in it."

"You're probably right," Vivi said.

After Vivi got home, she spent some more time on her Greek report. Then her curiosity got the best of her. Was there perhaps *another* note in that book she was returning tomorrow? One more note still clinging inside that book she had shaken out so carefully?

Maybe one more note would solve the puzzle. Maybe it would tell Vivi something important.

Vivi started flipping through the book, and then she shook it again. *Bingo!* One more note fluttered to the floor. For a moment, Vivi stared at the violet illustration. Then she bent down and snatched it up.

This note was written to someone named Puck.

How sweet it was when you and I went to Paris...it seems a hundred years ago, Puck. Has it been that long since I was happy? My life is so miserable. How could I have married someone I now hate so much? Oh, Puck, what fools we mortals be, or something! M

Vivi put the note on her desk. In spite of herself, she was being drawn into the mystery. She really hadn't wanted to get involved. But she couldn't help it now. She began to imagine Melissa's life. Here was a lovely but unhappy wife, married to a wretch who perhaps killed her. Puck must have been an old boyfriend.

It was getting late, but the light was

still on in Vivi's room. Even though she was very tired, Vivi sorted through the pages again, searching for one more clue.

Then Mom came to the door. "Vivi? You've got classes early tomorrow morning, don't you? You should be in bed," she said crossly.

"I've been working on a report for school," Vivi lied, "but I'm done now, Mom. I'm going to bed right away."

"Well, you better. If you don't get your sleep you'll end up sick, and then your education and everything else goes down the drain," Mom scolded.

Vivi found the last note just then, between the last pages of the history book.

> I am leaving my husband. I simply cannot stand it anymore. The boredom, the stupidity....M

Maybe, Vivi thought, that was what caused her death. Her husband *knew* he was losing her!

Chapter 5

During her classes all the next morning, Vivi was thinking about Melissa. What she had done gave her a spooky feeling. She had peered into a dead woman's sad life and come across what might be clues to her murder.

What if Barry Foster *was* the man in the library? It would have been easy to get rid of his bushy beard and long hair. Was it grief and guilt that had turned his eyes into such dark, burning searchlights?

What if he had gotten away with murder?

Vivi wondered if she had been right to put the notes back in the book. And was it really a good idea to return the book to the strange man this afternoon?

Was she helping him hide his crime?

Of course Vivi was eager to give the man the two books, just to be done with him. But still she agonized over the decision. Maybe she should have sent the notes to the police.

After her last class ended, Vivi removed the notes from her binder. Then she headed for the library.

The man was waiting for her when she walked into the history section. Immediately she handed him the two books he had asked for. "Here they are," she said. But when she turned to go, he grabbed her arm.

"Wait just a moment, please," he said in his very pleasant, normal sounding voice. For sure, his appearance was haggard and frightening, but he *did* have a beautiful voice. "How long have you been taking out books on Greece from this library?"

"Oh, just a couple of days," Vivi lied. Actually, it had been more than a week.

"I found that quite a number of books on Greece had been checked out recently—all in the past week or ten days," the man said. "Are you *sure* you didn't check them out?"

"No, no, I *didn't*! Just these," Vivi stammered, growing more nervous by the minute. "I've got to go now. . . . "

He held her arm and said, "Please forgive me. If you'll just give me one more moment. Have you found anything in the books? Ah . . . things that don't really belong there, you know. Perhaps letters . . . notes . . . cards?" he asked.

"What?" Vivi played dumb. "I just found a couple dead bugs. Of course, I didn't go through every page. I just read the chapters I needed for my report."

The man then looked directly into Vivi's eyes. "I don't believe you are telling me the entire truth," he said. "I think perhaps you did find something. You *did*, didn't you?"

"No," Vivi mumbled, "I didn't find

anything. Now please let go of my arm."

"But I *need* whatever you found. I know that you are a very young woman who probably has romantic notions. Perhaps you found something that was interesting or amusing to you, but you must give whatever you found to me!" The man's voice grew heated. "People put important things into books for safekeeping. Sometimes the books are mistakenly given away. That is what happened in this instance. So, you *must* give me whatever it is you found!"

"I *told* you I didn't find anything," Vivi said, her voice rising in fear.

The librarian looked up sharply. "Is everything all right, miss?" she called.

"Yes," Vivi said, pulling her arm from the man's loosening grasp. Now she bitterly regretted keeping the notes in her school binder. They didn't mean anything to her. But she was a poor liar, and now she had aroused this strange man's suspicions. It was too late. He *knew* that she had something he wanted. If she gave them back to him now, he would know for sure she had lied. Then he would think she was holding back even more. Suddenly Vivi turned numb. She had the notes he was searching for, and *he knew where she lived.*

When Vivi got home at last, she raced to Jamal's apartment.

"I'm in a big mess," she wailed. "I kept those notes that I found in the book about Crete. And now that weird guy in the library is suspicious of me! It was like he knew very well that I was lying when I told him I didn't have anything."

"You got to keep out of this, girl," Jamal said worriedly. Then he looked at his watch. "Tell you what. The library is still open. Have you got the notes with you now?"

"Yeah, " Vivi said.

"We'll hurry over there and stick the notes in any old Greek book donated by that rich lady, Lulu. Then you don't go back to that library for a long time, you hear me?" Jamal said seriously.

Vivi nodded. Right now she just wanted to get rid of Melissa's notes. They were too dangerous to keep.

Vivi and Jamal hurried through the early evening mist toward the library. It shouldn't take but a few minutes, Vivi thought. They'd just find *any* old Greek book that Ms. Foster had donated, stick the notes in it, and head out.

Vivi and Jamal hurried into the library, but before they'd gone more than a few feet, the man they feared confronted them. "Please," he said in his nice, polite voice, "could we step outside for a moment to talk?"

With big strong Jamal at her side, Vivi wasn't afraid, so the two teenagers stepped out into the twilight.

"I need to tell you who I am and what this is all about," the man said.

"Okay," Vivi said.

"I'm a police detective," he said. "I'm

working on a series of really tough, unsolved murder cases. Right now I'm investigating the death of Melissa Foster. We have reason to believe that she placed incriminating notes and letters in some old books—books that were later donated to the library. That's why it's so important for me to get my hands on all that material. Do you understand?"

"Yes," Vivi said, trembling in spite of her effort to remain calm. Who was he trying to kid? His story *couldn't* be true! The man looked so awful, so threatening! She didn't believe him for a minute.

If he had *really* been conducting a police investigation, he would have sent uniformed officers to confiscate all the books that might contain evidence. Surely, the police wouldn't have sent a wretched fellow like this sneaking around and paging through library books.

Chapter 6

"Can you now understand why your cooperation is so important?" the man asked.

"Yes, but I've already given you all you wanted," Vivi said.

The man looked at Jamal. "Is this young woman your girlfriend?" he asked.

"Yes, sir, she sure is," Jamal said with a grin. "She's my lady."

"Well, you wouldn't want anything to happen to her, I'm sure. Wouldn't it be terrible if something unfortunate happened to her—like what happened to poor Melissa Foster? We are afraid the man who killed Melissa is still out there. When Melissa was pushed down the stairs, she suffered a broken neck. That lovely young woman was loved—just as you love this girl here! It's not right that her murderer got away. I'm sure you can see that," the man said in an emotional voice.

"What did you say your name was, sir?" Jamal asked in a stern voice. He didn't believe the guy either.

"My name? Detective Ed Smith," the man said.

"Well, Detective Smith, the thing of it is, my lady here doesn't know a thing about all this stuff, okay? She's just a little college girl doing a project on the Greeks. She doesn't know a thing about any notes or letters or murders, okay? So, good luck to you on your investigation. But I don't want you bothering this lady anymore, okay?" Jamal's voice was harsh.

The man just stood there, as if in shock. He grew even paler than he was before, then turned and walked away.

"Come on," Jamal said to Vivi. "Let's

go in the library and put that stupid stuff back in a couple of books."

Vivi stuffed the notes into a big book on Sparta. Then she put the book back on the shelf in the stacks.

"Let's get out of here now, Vivi," Jamal said, "and no more looking in Greek books—not *here*, anyway! I don't know what that guy's problem is, but he sure ain't no cop. He's probably some nut with a dull life who wants to be part of something important. The first time he stumbled on a note in a book, he remembered the death of this lady. That's what got his imagination going!"

"But Jamal, the notes and letters . . . they *do* seem like evidence," Vivi said. "I wonder if the police *are* looking into that death anymore. Maybe we should tell them about what I found."

"We don't even know if those notes are real. Maybe this weirdo wrote them and planted them himself. Maybe he was browsing in the library one day and read an old newspaper story about Melissa Foster's mysterious death. Doesn't that make sense? I'm telling you, he just wove a *fantasy* about it! The important thing is, it's got nothing to do with us, Vivi. You know what curiosity did to the cat, don't you, girl?" Jamal reminded her.

But, in spite of everything Jamal said, Vivi couldn't get the strange man off her mind. At the end of the week she caught a bus and a trolley to a library at the other end of town. She went to the old newspapers that had been transferred to microfilm. Soon she was sitting before a screen, looking at news stories about the death of Melissa Foster.

Photos of Melissa showed a slim, fashionably dressed young woman. Barry Foster appeared as a well-muscled college football player, then as a man with long hair and beard. Vivi didn't think the man who called himself Ed Smith could really be Barry Foster—but she couldn't be absolutely sure.

The news stories described the night Melissa had fallen down the flight of stairs. It was just after a dinner party at the mansion where she lived with her husband. She had suffered a broken neck and died hours later at the hospital. Mr. Foster, her husband, claimed to have been napping in their upstairs bedroom when she fell. Blood tests showed that Melissa had drunk a cocktail, but she was not intoxicated.

One of the stories mentioned marital difficulties between the Fosters. Melissa was seeing a lawyer about filing for divorce. Barry Foster had a million-dollar life insurance policy on his wife. His computer business had filed for bankruptcy the year before, so he was presumed to be in financial trouble. The motive seemed clear enough: Barry Foster hurled his wife down the long flight of stairs because their marriage was over, and he wanted her money.

But the police had never arrested him

because there was no solid evidence.

Vivi left the library feeling sick. She felt so sorry for Melissa Foster. What if the young wife really *had* been murdered by her wicked husband? Vivi remembered the chilling words on the violet-decorated notepaper:

How much longer must I suffer? He will be the death of me yet. . . . Oh, what a bed of pain I have made for myself!

Vivi was torn with guilt. If Barry Foster had killed his wife, he should be paying for it. Now she was ashamed that she hadn't turned the notes over to the police. The pretty young face of Melissa Foster haunted her mind.

Chapter 7

Vivi had dinner that night at Jamal's apartment. While they were doing the dishes, she asked Jamal's mother if she knew anything about the Melissa Foster case. There was a good chance Mrs. Grey might remember something from all the newspaper articles and TV reports at the time.

"Oh, we were all following it," Mrs. Grey laughed. "It wasn't no 'crime of the century,' but it was interesting enough to grab the attention of this city. You kids were only eight or nine years old then— but lots of us followed the story like it was a soap opera!"

"So, did anybody ever say what happened to Barry Foster afterward, Ma?" Jamal asked. "What did the dude do after he lost his lady?"

"Foster collected on the insurance and went off to Europe, as I recall. I read a story that said he was grieving real bad for his wife. Maybe it was guilt. It always seemed to me that he pushed her down those stairs," Mrs. Grey said.

"Hmmm . . . I wonder where he is now," Vivi said.

"Who knows? I haven't read a thing about him for a long time. Maybe he's not even alive. I remember the last picture of him that was in the paper. He looked like a different man. He wasn't stocky anymore. He was clean shaven and had a short haircut. He looked like a broken man. But I still say it could have been *guilt* that was eating him up!" Mrs. Grey said.

Vivi glanced at Jamal. The strange man in the library seemed to be haunted by something all right. Maybe he *was* Barry Foster. Maybe he still feared being tried for the murder of his wife. If he had somehow learned that her notes were hidden in the books, it made sense that he was desperately trying to retrieve them. After all, since he had never been tried for murder, it was still an open case. Whenever new evidence surfaced, he could still be tried for the crime.

As Mrs. Grey dished out servings of dessert, sweet potato pie, her eyes were bright with interest in the murder mystery. "That inexperienced young girl married a cold, hard man. Then, when she couldn't take it anymore and was fixing to leave him, he did away with her. That's what *I* think happened," she said confidently.

Vivi and Jamal told Mrs. Grey nothing about the notes and letters. Both were afraid she'd be frightened by the information. Without a doubt Jamal's mom would want everything turned over to the police.

All the following week, Vivi didn't see the mysterious man from the library.

She didn't go near the downtown library anymore, and he never came down her street as he had done that one time.

Then, as Vivi was leaving her job on Monday night around 6:30, the man appeared out of the darkness. He fell in step with her as she hurried to her car. "Miss, don't be alarmed," he said in his calm, deep voice. "I just want a quick word with you."

"*Go away!*" Vivi cried angrily. "Don't bother me anymore." She wasn't really afraid this time because the street was crowded with people.

"Please, give me just a few minutes," the man pleaded.

"Okay, I'll talk to you, but I need to go home in just a minute," Vivi said.

"I lied to you about being a police detective," he said. "I suppose you guessed that. I'm not a very good liar."

"You're right—I didn't believe you," Vivi said. She watched the people walking by, making sure to notice if the crowd started to thin out. No way would she be alone on a deserted street with this man.

"Miss, I have been going over those books very carefully. Suddenly I found more notes in books I had already been through. *I'm quite sure you put them there after reading them.* But I need to know for certain if that is what happened, and if you have other notes hidden at home," he said.

"Who are you?" Vivi demanded.

"I am a man who loved Melissa Foster very much. I know that she was killed, and I have been spending all these years trying to find justice for her! That is why you must turn over any notes or letters you still have," the man said earnestly.

"I don't *have* any letters or notes," Vivi insisted. Staring at the gaunt, pale face before her, she remembered one of the violet notes. It had referred to a man nicknamed *Puck.* Could this man be

Puck? Melissa had said that she and Puck had once gone to Paris together.

"All right, miss. I would ask you for one favor. Do not talk to anyone about the notes you read. Do not mention them to a soul. I am gathering all the evidence I will need against the man who killed Melissa. Then I will take it all to the district attorney. You must not say *anything*—or the murderer will be alerted that I am onto him. Don't you see? The case could be blown before I've had time to gather all the evidence!"

"I won't say anything to anybody," Vivi promised. "Believe me—I just want to forget this whole thing and get on with my own life."

"Good. That's all that I ask. I loved Melissa so very much. She was so beautiful and good. She was a rare treasure. Her death broke my heart. Still, I can hardly bear the thought that she's really gone," the man said, his grief-striken voice shaking with emotion.

Vivi was dying to ask this man if he was Puck, the former boyfriend that Melissa had described in her letter. But asking that question would be admitting that Vivi had read the notes. "I'm really sorry about what happened to Melissa. It's very sad," Vivi said, "but I must be going home now."

He reached out his icy fingers and grasped Vivi's hands. "I have your solemn promise, then? You will not speak a word of this to anyone? Do you cross your heart and hope to die?" As he spoke, his big dark eyes seemed to take fire, glowing in the darkness like a cat's eyes.

"I p-promise," Vivi said nervously as she pulled free of him and hurried toward her car. She looked back once and saw him standing on the sidewalk, staring at her.

Usually Vivi took the bus and trolley, but now she was grateful that she had driven to work that day. She could drive right home instead of waiting on the corner for the bus. She wanted to be away from there quickly! She breathed a sigh of relief when the engine turned over and her old blue car sprang into motion. As she drove away, the man stood looking after her.

Chapter 8

When Vivi rushed into her apartment, her brothers were getting ready to go to a friend's house for a sleepover. Just now they were hunched over something, reading it with great interest.

Pedro read it out loud with exaggerated drama:

Dear little Melissa, I am trying to rescue you from that ghastly place. Have courage! Puck

"*Pedro!*" Vivi cried. "Where did you get that?"

"From one of your old library books the other night. You left it lying there, and this paper fell out when I picked it up. Who's Melissa?" Pedro asked.

"I got one, too," Luis boasted. "Only

mine isn't mushy. It's ugly. Listen:

"I think he wants me dead so he can collect my insurance.

"I found an envelope, too. Only the guy's name isn't Puck. It's, uh . . . Bruce Burkett."

"Give me those letters," Vivi cried, snatching them from her brothers. Then their ride to the sleepover arrived and the boys went out, yelling and shouting.

Vivi took the letters to her room, her brain spinning with confusion and worry. She looked up Bruce Burkett in the phone book. There was just one listed, so she called his number. She was so nervous that she could hardly hold the phone and punch in the right numbers. But she was determined to find out what was going on.

"Hello," Vivi said to the man who answered. "This is Vivi Calderon calling. I was looking through some old books taken from Lulu Foster's collection in the downtown library. I came across some really strange notes from someone named 'M'. They were like cries for help. One note mentioned a guy named Puck—and there was an envelope with your name on it."

The man gasped. "Oh! After all this time! Melissa Foster and I were in acting school together. She called me Puck because I had once played that role. We were very close. Then she married—and became quite miserable. She told me she was hiding notes about her terrible life in her mother-in-law's books. She wanted the world to know what she'd been through in case her wretched husband killed her—which in the end he did! Later, I heard that those books went to the city library when old Mrs. Foster died. Oh, Ms. Calderon, could you send them to me?"

"Yes, but I have just two. This weird guy in the library got most of them," Vivi said.

"What guy?" Burkett asked in a

shocked, suspicious sounding voice.

"I don't know, just this really weird guy. He was flipping through the books real fast. He even followed me home and asked me if I had found anything in the books—like letters," Vivi said.

"What did this man look like?" Burkett asked.

"Uh . . . tall, skinny. Ordinary looking. He wore a good suit, but it was old. he was really pale and—"

Burkett cut into Vivi's words. "He had eyes like a bird of prey, right?"

"Yeah!" Vivi cried. "That's exactly right. His eyes gave me the creeps big time."

"It's Foster—Barry Foster," Burkett said in an alarmed voice.

"But it couldn't be! I mean, he didn't look like the big beefy guy in the newspaper pictures I saw," Vivi said.

"It's been ten years. Ten years of guilt and hiding out from people who know what he did—people who hate him for getting away with murder. That must take a toll," Burkett said. "Now he's terrified that the notes and letters might contain enough evidence to hang him! Miss, listen to me. If he knows where you live, you are in danger. Be very careful. This is a desperate, driven man. He is capable of anything. Look what he did to Melissa!"

Vivi felt numb. "I . . . I'll mail you the letters," she promised.

"Use express mail, Ms. Calderon, and I plead with you to be very, *very* careful. If you see Foster lurking around your home, call the police immediately. Don't delay," Burkett said.

When Vivi hung up the phone, she rushed downstairs to make sure the main door of the apartment building was locked. Incoming tenants all had a special key, but sometimes they were careless and left the doors open for convenience.

"Rats!" Vivi grumbled, finding the

door open. Quickly closing and locking it, she went back upstairs. She had to write a paper on F. Scott Fitzgerald's *The Great Gatsby* for her American lit class tomorrow.

After about five minutes, Vivi heard someone at the apartment door. This visitor didn't knock or anything. The bell didn't ring. But someone very quietly tried the door. Luckily, it was locked. But even the *thought* that someone might be out there in the hall, trying her doorknob, made Vivi cringe in terror.

Chapter 9

Then it suddenly hit Vivi that she was alone in the apartment. Mom would be working until 9 tonight, two hours from now. Her brothers were spending the night at a friend's house.

Vivi's legs grew weak. Maybe she hadn't heard anybody try the door at all, she thought. Or maybe some kid from down the hall was playing around, trying all the doors. Vivi went to the door and looked out the peephole. No one was there. Smiling nervously, she told herself it was just her imagination.

Vivi returned to her book, but her mind was on Mr. Burkett. She was anxious to get those two letters to him tomorrow. He sounded like a nice, normal man. No doubt he had genuinely loved Melissa before she had married Barry Foster. What a heartache it must have been for him to know how unhappy Melissa was—and then to hear of her violent death.

It felt spooky being in the house all by herself. Vivi decided to turn on the TV. She often studied best with some kind of background noise.

"Let's see," Vivi said to herself, flipping through the television guide. "I'll turn on some old sitcom to keep me company." After she clicked on the TV, she returned to her book. She wished Jamal would come over to keep her company. He often came over at night, especially when Vivi's brothers were spending the night with their friends. It was quiet then—a real relief to get rid of the little pests. But at the moment, Vivi would have welcomed even the company of her noisy brothers.

After about 15 minutes, Vivi decided to call Jamal. Maybe he was home from work. He'd be glad to come over if Vivi asked him. She sure needed some company right now!

Vivi picked up the phone and noticed that the familiar buzz of the dial tone was missing. She stared at the phone. It was dead! But it was *never* dead. Vivi had always taken it for granted that anytime she needed to use the phone, it would be there for her. She ran to the phone in the bedroom. It was dead, too!

"The phone is dead," Vivi said aloud, although there was nobody in the apartment to hear her. "I'll have to report that it's out of order. I'll call from a neighbor's. . . ."

Vivi started across the room toward the door, but then she stopped. An old lady, Ms. Pennington, lived next door. She'd gladly let Vivi use her phone to report that the Calderons' phone was out of order. But did Vivi dare to step out into the hall? What if *he* was there, waiting for her? What if he had tried the door and found it locked? What if he was just waiting for Vivi to appear so he could force his way into the apartment?

Mr. Burkett's dire warnings flashed in Vivi's mind.

She stared at the locked door, her breath now coming in short little gasps. She was trapped on the second floor of an apartment building—cut off from the rest of the world!

Now it dawned on Vivi that Barry Foster probably had disabled her phone line so she couldn't get help!

Vivi rushed to the window. Maybe she could open it and yell for somebody to call the police. Maybe someone down on the street would hear her. Or perhaps Ms. Pennington had her windows open. A neighbor that close could surely hear Vivi yelling. Except that Ms. Pennington was deaf. . . .

Vivi looked through the peephole again. But again, she saw nothing. Then it occurred to her! She could only see directly in front of the door. If he was standing off to one side, she couldn't see him through the peephole.

As Vivi was standing at the door, wondering what to do, she saw the doorknob begin to slowly turn. Someone was tinkering with the lock! She felt paralyzed. Vivi dreaded looking out the peephole for fear that her worst fears would be confirmed. But she had to find out who was out there.

"*You!*" she screamed, seeing Barry Foster. "What are you doing here?"

The man managed a thin smile. "Oh, please don't be alarmed. I just want to ask if you found anymore notes or letters. I came to retrieve them. Please let me in for a few minutes."

"My father is sleeping in the bedroom," Vivi cried, "and if I wake him up, he'll be really furious at you. "

"Dear girl, you *have* no father. And I've seen your mother coming home from work some time after nine. I assume she's putting in a lot of overtime at night. This evening I saw your brothers leaving with a suitcase. So I doubt there is anyone there but you. Just let me in for a few minutes," he said. "I assure you I am quite harmless."

"Unless you beat it, I'm calling the police," Vivi cried.

"Alas, I don't believe your phone is working just now," the man said.

"*You* messed with it, didn't you?" Vivi gasped. "Listen, I'm going to the window right now and yell my head off. Somebody will hear me, and you can bet that the police will come!"

But the doorknob began to turn even more forcefully. He was on the verge of breaking in! There was no more time. At any moment Barry Foster could fling open the door and burst in!

Vivi whirled around and rushed to the window. She had to get out of there before he got in. The only escape route she saw was out the window and down the fire escape. She was afraid of scrambling down the rickety old fire escape, but there was no other way.

Sliding the window open, Vivi quietly forced the screen out. But just as she did, she heard the door open. Her whole body began to shake as she scrambled out across the window sill, jumped on the fire escape, and started climbing down to the street.

As she neared the bottom of the fire escape, she saw Foster looking down at her from the window. He swung his long legs out. He was coming after her! Vivi's heart was pounding as her feet hit the street. She started screaming—but the streets were deserted now, and the loud rumble of rap music from somebody's open window was drowning out most of the other city noise.

Chapter 10

Down on the street, Barry Foster quickly caught up to the girl, his pincer-like hand closing on her wrist. He dragged her down an alley and shoved her through the door of what appeared to be a grimy basement apartment.

"Help!" Vivi screamed, but nobody seemed to hear her.

Foster kicked the door shut behind them and said, "Stop yelling! Calm down! I only want what is mine. This is all your fault, you foolish girl! Why did you have to meddle in my business and cause all this trouble?"

Vivi heard police sirens screaming in the distance. Had someone seen her struggling with Foster in the alley? Were the police on their way—or were they going somewhere else? "I never took your letters," Vivi cried.

"Do you know who I am?" he asked her grimly, twisting her arm.

"Yes, you're Barry Foster," Vivi said.

"Do you know what my life has been like for the ten years since my wife died?" he asked in an anguished voice. "I lost my wife. I lost all my money. I lost my friends and the respect of everyone who had ever known me. When my mother died three years ago, I was totally alone. Because of the evil lies my wife told about me, they all think I killed her!"

Vivi stared silently at the man. The police sirens seemed to be getting closer. She hoped against hope that they were coming *here*. If only someone had seen Foster push her into this miserable little apartment!

"Melissa *hated* me," the man groaned. "She lied about me. Then she put vile notes in all of my mother's books. I didn't know she was doing that. She knew that Mother's library was destined to be a gift to the city on her death—so Melissa put her notes where they would surely be found someday. Don't you see? She's reached out of the grave to destroy me! That's why you must give me all those incriminating letters and notes. I have to burn them once and for all," he raved, apparently oblivious to the sound of the approaching sirens.

Barry Foster had now lost it completely. He was obviously deranged by ten years of guilt and fear. Now, his voice lowered to a rasping whisper, "I never killed her. We were arguing at the top of the stairs. She was mocking me and jeering at me. I . . . I slapped her face. I had never done that before, I swear. But, somehow, she lost her balance and fell. . . ."

Then he raised his arms and clamped his hands over his ears as if to shut out an unbearable sound. "I can still hear the thump of her body tumbling down the stairs. Her head hit the stone jar at the bottom, and . . . I knew she was dead. I didn't know what to do. I rushed upstairs and changed into my pajamas. When the maid found her, I pretended I'd been asleep when she fell. *But I never killed her.* It was an accident. . . . "

The police sirens faded now. Vivi was horrified. The cop cars were going somewhere else! The wailing sounds became fainter and fainter before trailing away in the night.

"You read most of the notes and letters, didn't you?" Foster demanded. "You're just like the rest of them. You think I murdered Melissa, and you intend to take your little stash of evidence to the police. That's your plan, isn't it?"

"No! You've got it all wrong!" Vivi cried. Her gaze was fixed desperately on the door—it was so close! The man was distracted by emotion. Perhaps she could take him by surprise and make a run for it. "I swear that I won't tell anybody anything."

"*Liar!*" Foster cried. "You are nothing but a liar. I can read your deceitful intentions in your face."

Vivi noticed an old lamp nearby, a tarnished but expensive lamp covered with cobwebs. Although Barry Foster had long since lost his expensive lifestyle, this lamp was apparently a remnant of the past. Now Vivi snatched it up, pulling out the plug and casting the room into darkness. It had been the only source of light in the tiny, dirty room. She hurled the lamp at Barry Foster, hoping to momentarily distract him so she could make it out the door.

Foster grasped at Vivi as she dashed by. He caught hold of her jacket, but Vivi pulled free, leaving him holding the jacket by its empty sleeve. She raced out into the dark alley.

This time when Vivi screamed,

several people appeared. Then somebody called the police, and by the time Vivi reached the end of the alley, a police car had arrived on the scene. She frantically flagged down the officer and cried out, "The guy who kidnapped me is in there!" pointing to Foster's apartment.

After Barry Foster was taken away, a police officer took the shaken girl back to her apartment. A few minutes later, Mrs. Calderon came home from work. Vivi told her mother everything that had happened. Mrs. Calderon shook her head in amazement. "Girl, how do you get mixed up in such things?" she cried. "Well, I'm just grateful that you're okay, baby."

Vivi grinned and said, "Well, Mom, you're always saying I should get a good education. If I hadn't been in the library looking for those books on Greece, none of this would have happened!"

In the school library that day, Vivi had downloaded one of the newspaper photos of Melissa Foster. Before she climbed into bed that night, she looked again at the beautiful young woman. What had *really* happened to her?

Vivi still didn't know if Barry Foster had killed her by accident or on purpose. But now she breathed a deep sigh of relief. Nobody who had seen Foster's tortured face could say that he had gotten away with anything. There was some satisfaction in that.

COMPREHENSION QUESTIONS

RECALL

1. How did Vivi discover that the strange man from the library had followed her home?

2. What was hidden inside the library books Vivi brought home?

3. What had happened to Melissa Foster?

4. What lie did Barry Foster tell Vivi about his identity and purpose?

VOCABULARY

1. Vivi became more and more curious about Melissa Foster's "cryptic notes." What does the word *cryptic* mean?

2. Vivi noticed that the strange man had a "terrible pallor about him." What is *pallor*?

3. Lulu Margaret Foster identified herself as a "Grecophile." What is a *Grecophile*?

IDENTIFYING CHARACTERS

1. Which character was a "patron of the arts"?

2. Which character was Melissa's former boyfriend?

3. Which character had to write a paper comparing two Greek civilizations?

4. Which character suggested to Jamal that something "unfortunate" could happen to Vivi?

5. Which character told Vivi and Jamal all the details of the unsolved murder case?

DRAWING CONCLUSIONS

1. What two conclusions did Vivi's brothers draw about the man who was watching their apartment?

2. What conclusion did Vivi draw when she read Melissa's note to Puck?

3. What conclusion did Bruce Burkett draw about the strange man who was following Vivi?